FOR STEPHANIE FROM COUSIN B.

*Frederick Warne has a continuing commitment to reproduce Beatrix Potter's
exquisite watercolours to the highest possible standard. In 1993 and 1994,
taking advantage of the latest advances in printing technology and expertise, entirely new film
was made from her original book illustrations. The drawings are now reproduced with a quality
and a degree of authenticity never before attainable in print.*

FREDERICK WARNE

Published by the Penguin Group
27 Wrights Lane, London W8 5TZ, England
Penguin Books USA Inc., 375 Hudson Street New York, N. Y. 10014, USA
Penguin Books Australia Ltd, Ringwood, Victoria, Australia
Penguin Books Canada Ltd, 10 Alcorn Avenue, Toronto, Ontario, Canada M4V 3B2
Penguin Books (NZ) Ltd, 182-190 Wairau Road, Auckland 10, New Zealand

Penguin Books Ltd, Registered Offices: Harmondsworth, Middlesex, England

First published 1906 by Frederick Warne
This edition with new reproductions of Beatrix Potter's
book illustrations first published 1997

ISBN 0 7232 4301 8

Colour reproductions by
Saxon Photolitho Ltd. Norwich
Printed and bound in Great Britain by
William Clowes Limited, Beccles and London

0797

THE TALE OF
MR. JEREMY FISHER

❂

BY BEATRIX POTTER

FREDERICK WARNE

ONCE upon a time there was a frog called Mr. Jeremy Fisher; he lived in a little damp house amongst the buttercups at the edge of a pond.

THE water was all slippy-sloppy in the larder
and in the back passage.

But Mr. Jeremy liked getting his feet wet;
nobody ever scolded him, and he never
caught a cold!

HE was quite pleased when he looked out and saw large drops of rain, splashing in the pond—

"I will get some worms and go fishing and catch a dish of minnows for my dinner," said Mr. Jeremy Fisher. "If I catch more than five fish, I will invite my friends Mr. Alderman Ptolemy Tortoise and Sir Isaac Newton. The Alderman, however, eats salad."

MR. JEREMY put on a macintosh, and a pair of shiny goloshes; he took his rod and basket, and set off with enormous hops to the place where he kept his boat.

THE boat was round and green, and very
like the other lily-leaves. It was tied to a
water-plant in the middle of the pond.

MR. JEREMY took a reed pole, and pushed the boat out into open water. "I know a good place for minnows," said Mr. Jeremy Fisher.

Mr. Jeremy stuck his pole into the mud and fastened his boat to it.

THEN he settled himself cross-legged and arranged his fishing tackle. He had the dearest little red float. His rod was a tough stalk of grass, his line was a fine long white horse-hair, and he tied a little wriggling worm at the end.

THE rain trickled down his back, and for nearly an hour he stared at the float.

"This is getting tiresome, I think I should like some lunch," said Mr. Jeremy Fisher.

He punted back again amongst the water-plants, and took some lunch out of his basket.

"I will eat a butterfly sandwich, and wait till the shower is over," said Mr. Jeremy Fisher.

A GREAT big water-beetle came up underneath the lily leaf and tweaked the toe of one of his goloshes.

Mr. Jeremy crossed his legs up shorter, out of reach, and went on eating his sandwich. Once or twice something moved about with a rustle and a splash amongst the rushes at the side of the pond.

"I trust that is not a rat," said Mr. Jeremy Fisher; "I think I had better get away from here."

MR. JEREMY shoved the boat out again a
little way, and dropped in the bait. There
was a bite almost directly; the float gave a
tremendous bobbit!

"A minnow! a minnow! I have him by the
nose!" cried Mr. Jeremy Fisher, jerking up
his rod.

BUT what a horrible surprise! Instead of a smooth fat minnow, Mr. Jeremy landed little Jack Sharp the stickleback, covered with spines!

The stickleback floundered about the boat, pricking and snapping until he was quite out of breath. Then he jumped back into the water.

AND a shoal of other little fishes put their heads out, and laughed at Mr. Jeremy Fisher.

AND while Mr. Jeremy sat disconsolately on the edge of his boat—sucking his sore fingers and peering down into the water—a *much* worse thing happened; a really *frightful* thing it would have been, if Mr. Jeremy had not been wearing a macintosh!

A GREAT big enormous trout came up—
ker-pflop-p-p-p! with a splash—and it seized
Mr. Jeremy with a snap, "Ow! Ow! Ow!"—
and then it turned and dived down to the
bottom of the pond!

But the trout was so displeased with the
taste of the macintosh,
that in less than
half a minute it
spat him out
again; and the
only thing it
swallowed
was Mr.
Jeremy's
goloshes.

MR. JEREMY bounced up to the surface of the water, like a cork and the bubbles out of a soda water bottle; and he swam with all his might to the edge of the pond.

He scrambled out on the first bank he came to, and he hopped home across the meadow with his macintosh all in tatters.

"WHAT a mercy that was not a pike!" said Mr. Jeremy Fisher. "I have lost my rod and basket; but it does not much matter, for I am sure I should never have dared to go fishing again!"

HE put some sticking plaster on his fingers,
and his friends both came to dinner. He
could not offer them fish, but he had
something else in his larder.

SIR ISAAC NEWTON wore his black and
gold waistcoat,

AND Mr. Alderman Ptolemy Tortoise
brought a salad with him in a string bag.

AND instead of a nice dish of minnows—
they had a roasted grasshopper with lady-bird
sauce; which frogs consider a beautiful treat;
but *I* think it must have been nasty.

THE END